Teachers

BY CECILIA MINDEN

Published by The Child's World®
1980 Lookout Drive • Mankato, MN 56003-1705
800-599-READ • www.childsworld.com

Acknowledgments
The Child's World®: Mary Berendes, Publishing Director
The Design Lab: Design
Jody Jensen Shaffer: Editing
Pamela J. Mitsakos: Photo Research

Photos
Alexander Raths/123RF.com: 10-11; BrandXPictures:
pencil; Cindy Chiu: 9, 16; Dragonimages/Dreamstime.
com: 12; GlobalStock/iStock.com: 4; iStock/
Thinkstock.com: 6-7; Jupiterimages/Thinkstock.com:
18; kali9/iStock.com: 14; michaeljung/Shutterstock.
com: cover, 1; Monkey Business Images/Dreamstime.
com: 5; omgimages/iStock.com: 8; Photodisc:
crayons, letters, slate; Pressmaster/Shutterstock.com:
17; StHelena/iStock.com: 20-21

ISBN 9781626870185
LCCN 2013947392

Printed in the United States of America
Mankato, MN
December, 2013
PA02191

ABOUT THE AUTHOR

Dr. Cecilia Minden is a university professor and reading specialist with classroom and administrative experience in grades K–12. She earned her PhD in reading education from the University of Virginia.

CONTENTS

Hello, My Name Is Maria.

Hello. My name is Maria. Many people live and work in my neighborhood. Each of them helps the neighborhood in different ways.

I thought of all the things I like to do. I like to go to school. I like helping others learn new skills. How could I help my neighborhood when I grow up?

Do you like helping others learn?

I Could Be a Teacher!

Teachers enjoy learning. They know a lot about many different subjects. Teachers are good at helping students build new skills.

Best of all, teachers get to help others learn!

When Did This Job Start?
The first school in the United States to train new teachers opened in 1823. It was in Concord, Vermont. Nearly every state had such schools by 1900. Today, almost every university has a school of education to train new teachers.

Perhaps you would make a good teacher!

Learn About This Neighborhood Helper!

The best way to learn is to ask questions. Words such as *who*, *what*, *where*, *when*, and *why* will help me learn about being a teacher.

Where Can I Learn More?
National Association for the Education of Young Children
1509 16th Street NW
Washington, DC 20036

Recruiting New Teachers, Inc.
385 Concord Avenue, Suite 103
Belmont, MA 02478

Asking a teacher questions will help you learn more about the job.

Who Can Become a Teacher?

Girls and boys who enjoy learning and helping others may want to become teachers. There are many different kinds of teachers. They help others learn from kindergarten all the way through college. Teachers are important helpers in the neighborhood. They teach people how to read, write, solve problems, and learn new skills.

How Can I Explore This Job?

Ask your teacher about his job! Where did he go to school? How did he decide to become a teacher? What does he like best about teaching?

Teachers help people of all ages learn new skills.

Meet a Teacher!

This is Cindy Chiu. Her students call her Miss Chiu. She is a reading teacher at a school in Arlington, Virginia. Miss Chiu teaches children

How Many Teachers Are There?
About 3,800,000 people work as teachers.

Miss Chiu enjoys helping her students learn how to read.

how to become better readers and writers. When Miss Chiu is not in the classroom, she likes to swim, play tennis, read books, and write in her journal.

Teachers answer students' questions.

Where Can I Learn to Be a Teacher?

Teachers usually go to college. They take classes in many subjects because they have to help students learn many different things. Most teachers have to take a special test to get a teaching license. Teachers never stop learning. They sometimes take classes in the summer while students are on vacation!

How Much School Will I Need?

Public school teachers must have a four-year college degree. They must also take teacher training classes. Many states require education past college. Teachers must pass tests given by the state where they live. They are then given a license so they can work.

Teachers usually take a variety of college classes.

What Does a Teacher Need to Do the Job?

Miss Chiu loves books! She has many books for her students to read. Miss Chiu often uses a **dry erase board** when she is teaching.

Sometimes Miss Chiu's students have writing projects. She asks them to share what they write. Students take turns sitting in a chair called the Author's Chair. There they read what they wrote to the other children in the class.

What Are Some Tools I Will Use?
- Books
- Computer
- Dry erase board / markers
- Internet
- Paper
- Pen or pencil

What Clothes Will I Wear?

For men:
- Dress shirt or sweater
- Slacks

For women:
- Blouse or sweater
- Slacks

It is helpful for both men and women teachers to wear comfortable shoes.

Many schools feature computer labs.

Where Does a Teacher Work?

Miss Chiu's school has several classrooms, a gym for sports, and a playground for recess. There is also a computer lab and a library stacked with books for the children to read.

Miss Chiu usually comes to school early in the morning. She meets with other teachers to think of fun activities for the students. Miss Chiu meets with younger students later in the morning. She teaches these students how to read.

What's It Like Where I'll Work?
Teachers usually work in classrooms. These are clean and well-lighted. Sometimes teachers work outdoors. They watch children on the playground and during outdoor field trips.

How Much Money Will I Make?

Most teachers make between $40,000 and $45,000 a year.

Miss Chiu works with older children in the afternoon. They already know how to read. She helps them to become better readers. The students leave in the afternoon, but most teachers stay after school to attend meetings and to get their classroom ready for the next day.

Miss Chiu helps children develop their reading skills.

Who Works with Teachers?

Many people work with Miss Chiu at school. They include a principal, a librarian, a nurse, a coach, a secretary, a bus driver, a **custodian**, volunteers, and others who want to help the students learn.

What other Jobs Might I Like?
- Librarian
- Library media specialist
- Principal
- Recreation worker
- Teacher's aide

Librarians and teachers work together to show students that reading can be fun.

Many teachers use their free time to help students perform in a Reader's Theater.

When Is a Teacher a Director?

Teachers work doesn't always take place inside a classroom. They often help students with **extracurricular** activities. Miss Chiu and her students like to perform in a Reader's Theater. The students choose a favorite book and make a play using the characters from the book. They practice a lot. They like to perform their play for family and friends. Miss Chiu uses a video camera to record the play. She sends copies of the recording home to parents who were not able to come to the play.

How Might My Job Change?
Some teachers go on to become principals, counselors, and library media specialists.

I Want to Be a Teacher!

I think being a teacher would be a great way to be a neighborhood helper. Someday you may see me at the front of a classroom!

Is This Job Growing?
The need for teachers will grow as fast as other jobs.

Why Don't You Try Being a Teacher?

Do you think you would like to be a teacher? Why don't you create a how-to book? How-to books have instructions that show people how to do different things. You could teach someone how to tell a joke, make a peanut butter sandwich, jump rope, or whatever you know how to do. See the next page for instructions.

Maybe one day you'll help kids in your neighborhood learn.

Materials: pencils, crayons, markers, paper, stapler

Steps:

1. Think about something you can teach others.
2. Make a list of all the materials you need.
3. Write out the instructions, step by step.
4. Copy each step of the instructions on a separate paper.
5. Draw a picture for each step to show the reader what to do.
6. Put the pictures and instructions, in order, between two pieces of colorful paper, and staple them together.

GLOSSARY

custodian (kus-TOH-dee-yun)
someone who cleans a building and
helps take care of it

dry erase board (DRY ee-RAYSS
BORD) a board covered with white,
glossy plastic that can be written on
with markers and later wiped clean

extracurricular (ek-struh-kuh-RIK-
yuh-lur) student activities that occur
after school or that don't make up
the main part of a child's studies

LEARN MORE
ABOUT TEACHERS

BOOKS

Hayward, Linda. *A Day in the Life
of a Teacher.* New York: Dorling
Kindersley, 2001.

Liebman, Daniel. *I Want to Be a
Teacher.* Toronto: Firefly Books, 2001.

Parks, Peggy J. *Teacher.* Farmington
Hills, MI: Kidhaven Press, 2003.

WEB SITES

Visit our home page for lots of links
about teachers:

www.childsworld.com/links

*Note to Parents, Teachers, and Librarians: We routinely
check our Web links to make sure they're safe, active
sites—so encourage your readers to check them out!*

INDEX

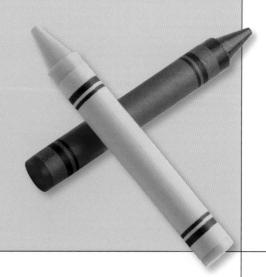